The Very Lonely Bathtub

Published by
M A G I N A T I O N   P R E S S
An Educational Publishing Foundation Book
American Psychological Association
750 First Street, NE
Washington, DC 20002

For more information about our books, including a complete catalog, please write to us,
call 1-800-374-2721, or visit our website at www.maginationpress.com.

Editor: Darcie Conner Johnston
Art Director: Susan K. White
The text type is Century Schoolbook
Printed by Phoenix Color, Rockaway, New Jersey

Library of Congress Cataloging-in-Publication Data

Rasmussen, Ann.
The very lonely bathtub / written by Ann Rasmussen and Marc Nemiroff ;
illustrated by Kate Flanagan.
p.   cm.
Summary: At first Claudia enjoys her new bathtub, which becomes in turn a fire engine,
a floating hospital, and a spaceship, but then she grows tired of being clean and
refuses to take a bath, no matter how dirty she gets.
ISBN 1-55798-607-X (alk. paper)
[1. Baths Fiction. 2. Cleanliness Fiction. 3. Behavior Fiction. 4. Imagination Fiction.]
I. Nemiroff, Marc A. II. Flanagan, Kate, ill. III. Title.
PZ7.R1819Vg 1999
99-36790
CIP

Manufactured in the United States of America
10 9 8 7 6 5 4 3 2 1

The Very Lonely Bathtub

WRITTEN BY
Ann Rasmussen and Marc Nemiroff

ILLUSTRATED BY
Kate Flanagan

MAGINATION PRESS • WASHINGTON, DC

For Nathan, Leah, Willie, and Gabriel, and all the
other children who ever needed a bath — AR and MN

For Molly, Fran, and Timothy — KF

Once upon a time...

not THAT long ago, maybe last summer, in a fancy bathtub shop on Main Street,

6

there was a simple bathtub with a very large heart.

This bathtub dreamed of keeping a nice family clean.
He wanted to live where there would be children
who would play in him,

and not just use him in a rush
like grown-ups did for boring old showers!

One Tuesday, Claudia and her parents came into the store. Her parents headed for the fancy and snobby bathtubs, the kind that wouldn't be fun to get clean in...

and the ones that acted
like they were big
swimming pools instead
of just bathtubs.

11

But Claudia raced straight to the humble tub,
shouting, "It's THIS one I want!
It's bright white and it smiles!"

So the tub became part of Claudia's family.

That very first night, Claudia
brought her bath toys into the tub
and played gleefully.
The tub's heart was filled with joy!
(Thank goodness he didn't overflow!)

Every night, the bathtub gurgled with pleasure at their play. Some nights he was a fire engine clanging through town, filled with water to put out fires.

Other nights he was a floating hospital
saving the sick and wounded.

Some nights he became
a spaceship, searching for
the Man in the Moon.

Other nights, he was a grand yacht
serving tea to the
Prince of Wales.

But one day…things changed.

Claudia proclaimed:
"NO MORE!"
She had grown tired of being clean.

She wouldn't take a bath no matter how much her parents pleaded and stared threateningly.

20

No matter how dirty she got.

The little tub became sad and lonely
and grew dull and lost his shine.

Claudia's parents called the tub doctor
(a plumber, they call it) who checked him all out.

22

The plumber shook his head and said,
"He works fine. All the faucets and pipes
and drains are in good working order.
But he hasn't been used much lately."

23

"You know, tubs don't have anyplace to go.
They're stuck to the floor,
just waiting for someone to play with them.
They can't run away to go find new friends!"

The plumber said, "Tubs have to have people,
especially children (who especially need
to get clean), to have fun with them.
This keeps them in good working order."

Claudia was watching and listening.
She started to think about being messy.
"All the fun of *getting* messy is gone if you're *already* messy!"

"And no one can stand how stinky I am
when I seesaw and swing in the park."

She remembered how cozy and calm
it felt to be squeaky-pink clean.

28

Then Claudia thought,
"When my tub is in good *working* order,
it keeps me in good *playing* order."

"I need to save my tub!"

At last Claudia understood
that her tub needed her
and she needed her tub.

She loved her dear tub
and knew that inside him
there was a great heart.

31

And so, from then on,
their adventures continued every single night.

(And Claudia stayed clean.)